Praise for
Annette: A Big, Hairy Mom

"*Annette: A Big, Hairy Mom* by John S. McFarland is a delightfully illustrated romp for young readers, woven together with legend, conspiracy theory, loveable monsters, colorful characters, and unforgettable character naming conventions such as Wesley Interruptus Buttinski. McFarland has the whimsical storytelling of Roald Dahl. A terrific book to read aloud with the kids."

~ Kevin M. Folliard, author of *Grayson North, Frost-Keeper of the Windy City*

"*Annette: A Big, Hairy Mom* is the kind of book every young Cryptid enthusiast should read. While so many films and books portray these beings as monstrous, the fact is they are more like us in many ways. Adventure, surprises, and discovery await the young mind in this delightful book. Recommended!"

~ David Bakara,
Expedition Bigfoot: The Sasquatch Museum,
Blue Ridge, Georgia

"All parts of *Annette: A Big, Hairy Mom* are scintillatingly believable in their sharp focus, realistic action, sure character, and plot development. Undoubtedly, like many readers, this reviewer was moved to tears when Evan sacrificed his beloved Froggums for Annette to cherish, understanding and identifying with her special loneliness. Like J.K. Rowling and others, McFarland never underestimates the sensitivity and sophistication of his intended audience."

~ Midwest Book Review

"Well, I must tell you: everybody loves Annette and I knew they would because it's just a lovely book. Young readers are excited by the story and many wan to read it again as soon as they finish it! They are very anxious to find out what happens in the next book!"

~Sanja Petriska, VF Libris

"I recently finished reading your book, Annette: A Big, Hairy Mom to my second grade class in the Parkway School District. My students loved your story! We used it in conjunction with our unit on chapter books...

"We thought Evan Nestor was very brave and rather intelligent, too. We also thought he was fortunate to have experienced such a thrilling adventure. His problems reminded some of us about times when we were lost and scared. Our class clapped when Evan Nestor was reunited with his parents.

"The students also loved Annette. Part of our class thought they might be afraid to read a story about a Sasquatch, but the cover put those fears to rest. Once we saw the illustration of Annette wearing the pink, heart-shaped sunglasses, we knew she was a good creature. Most of our group thought they would like to ride up on Annette's shoulders, the way Evan Nestor did. However, none of us wanted to stay in the trailer with crazy old Liam!...

"Thank you for writing such a wonderful story. It has been a long time since I have read a book that has captured the attention of my entire class. Looking forward to Annette's adventures as a grandmother!"

~ Mimi D. Barrow, Parkway School District, St. Louis County

ANNETTE:
A Big, Hairy Mom

Written and Illustrated by
John S. McFarland

From
Dark Owl Publishing, LLC

Arizona

Illustrations by John S. McFarland
Cover image by John S. McFarland
Cover design by Dark Owl Publishing, LLC

Visit us on our website at:
www.darkowlpublishing.com

More Young Readers Novels from
Dark Owl Publishing

Grayson North
Frost-Keeper of the Windy City
A totally cool urban fantasy adventure
by Kevin M. Folliard

Shivers, Scares, and Goosebumps
Short tales to chill you to your bones
by Vonnie Winslow Crist

In addition, all books from Dark Owl Publishing are
appropriate for at least teenagers to read.

Please see the Young Readers Bookstore page
on our website
for details on age appropriateness.

www.darkowlpublishing.com/the-yr-bookstore

For Great-Great Grandfather Larkin McFarland.
A Civil War veteran who,
along with his mule,
fought off one of these critters
in the woods one night:
one who was far less friendly than Annette.

Chapter 1

Tonight, like every night, Evan Nestor Bettancourt was hoping for monsters.

One night he had hoped so hard that a monster actually appeared in his room. Enormous, hairy and terrifying. He'd been so scared he was frozen in his bed like a wiper blade on his dad's windshield after an ice storm. From then on in his wishing, he had to make it clear that he didn't want real monsters. He was happy with imaginary ones in books. But it wasn't always up to him.

Even though Evan Nestor was the smallest second grader at Krantz's Grove Elementary, and he still liked to sleep with his stuffed frog Froggums, he suspected he was probably more grown up, not to mention smarter, than his friends at school. And he felt he was big enough to read his own story at bedtime. His mom and dad, though, still wanted to read to him every night. He had to admit that, most of the time, he looked forward to it, though he would never tell them.

Evan Nestor's parents disagreed on the subject of Froggums. His mom thought her son should keep his toy as long as he wanted it, but his dad did not.

"We have a twenty-dollars-off coupon at Toy Riot in Arcata, son," Dad said at dinner one night, "if you want to clear out some of these old things of yours. We could look at video games, or maybe a microscope. We could give Froggums and some of your other little

kid toys and books to the Krantz's Grove charity drive at the high school next week. Then younger kids from less fortunate families could enjoy them."

"*No!*" Evan Nestor interrupted. "Froggums is mine. My toys are mine! I want to keep them forever! It isn't my fault if poor people can't afford things. That doesn't mean they should get *my* things! We can give them money, or... coupons, but not my stuff!"

"All right, son," Evan Nestor's dad said with a wave of his hand. "We'll talk about it some other time."

"No Dad, we should never talk about it again. I want you to promise me we'll never talk about it again."

But now another bedtime had come, and Evan Nestor was scrubbed, his teeth brushed, and he was ready for sleep. He liked this time of the day, when he was clean and just a little tired, plopped in his bed and snug in his room. Everything was in its place: Plastic planets spun from his ceiling, and T-Rex and the Snow Monster, who he would never give up, watched him from the bookshelf.

He had already checked the Snow Monster, picked it up and turned it over in his hands, as he had done every night since the night it had come to life.

One night, in the middle of the winter when Evan Nestor was four years old, he awakened from a frightening dream to find the Snow Monster standing at his bedside, grinning at him. It was living, breathing, and twice the size of the biggest gorilla. So tall, in fact, it was touching the ceiling of his room. Evan Nestor was so terrified he could not move.

The Monster stared at him for the longest time, then shrugged as if to say, "If you aren't going to stop me, then I will do anything I want!" The Monster then began to pull clothes out of drawers, scatter toys across the floor, and eat Evan Nestor's macadamia nut cookie, which he had left unfinished on his nightstand.

Somehow, after all that, Evan Nestor had managed to fall back asleep, and when he excitedly told his parents about his adventure the next morning, his mom had said that it was Evan Nestor himself who had made a mess of his room. She pointed out that the half-eaten cookie was still on the nightstand where he had left it. This made Evan Nestor wonder if he had imagined the whole thing, or dreamed it. After a few days of thinking about it, he decided that it had really happened, and that he should keep a wary eye on this untrustworthy toy from now on.

So, for nearly four years, a close examination of the Snow Monster had become part of getting ready for bed. Tonight, as every other night, he could find nothing unusual about the toy that might make him suspicious.

Now Evan Nestor was ready for his story.

"Dad," he said, "can we have a story about Sinbad tonight? Or the Billy Goats Gruff? Or something about a giant?" He had been in a mood for a good giant story for a few days. The best thing about giants, in Evan Nestor's opinion, is that they are big and easy to see from a distance so they can't sneak up on you like a smaller monster could. That is, unless you fall asleep, as Evan Nestor himself had done, and let a monster surprise you. But he had learned to be cautious and would never let that happen again.

Evan Nestor's parents, of course, knew he loved stories with monsters in them, especially if the monsters were not too scary, but they disagreed about whether such stories were good for the boy. For Evan Nestor's part, he still had Froggums to hug when he needed to when the monsters were too frightening. Evan Nestor just couldn't imagine that Dad would want him to give Froggums away, especially when he suspected a monster or two were hiding in his drapes or under his bed or in his closet, waiting for his mom or dad to leave the room after putting him to bed. Hugging Froggums almost always worked, though he would never admit it to any of his friends. Even though he was smaller than them, he was smarter, and he didn't want them to know he still hugged a toy when he was frightened.

Evan Nestor's father smiled. "No, son. We haven't finished the volume about Vernon the Gnome talking about protoplasm yet. You want to hear how the book ends, don't you? We bought the Smarty-Pants series of science books for kids, and we should read them."

Evan Nestor's dad was named Duane Higs Bettancourt. He was forty years old and taught biology at Krantz's Grove High School. He wore thick glasses that never looked clean, and he always looked like an unmade bed or a pile of laundry. Duane, like Evan Nestor, had been an only child, but through reading and watching many educational films, he felt he had taught himself to be a very good and informed parent. Evan Nestor knew his dad had always believed that anything could be learned through reading. Perhaps for that reason, he had never traveled out of Northern California further than San Francisco. "Everything in the world you need," he always said, "is within twenty miles of you, so why go further?"

"Um, I guess so, Dad," Evan Nestor said. "But it's my story; why can't I have the one I want? Maybe we could give the Smarty-Pants books to charity."

"I don't like stories about monsters or make-believe animals," Duane said. "You need to start to learn the difference between made-up things and real things. Imagination has its place in life when you're young, but when you grow up you will forget all about these fairy stories.

"I have never felt very comfortable telling you

5

those, but you were little, so I agreed with your mom and went along. But now you're getting to be a bigger boy, and we should start just reading about real things."

Evan Nestor was puzzled. Did that mean Vernon the Gnome was real? Maybe he should start reading his own bedtime stories after all, he thought.

"There are no monsters or unknown animals," Duane went on. "These are modern, scientific times, son. I think people know all there is to know. Searching for new animals on land or in the sea is silliness, and doing any more scientific research with everything important already discovered is a waste of money. I want to teach you about the bacteria or nematodes I talk about in class—practical! They are practical creatures. And, in my opinion, more interesting than any monster or giant."

Evan Nestor's mom, Megan, dressed in her jogging outfit, was standing in the doorway of his bedroom, smiling a slight smile. Evan Nestor had blonde hair and blue eyes as she did, and she had heard this talk before, always smiling the same smile. He knew his mom was wondering if Duane was going to make his usual speech about how the U. S. Patent Office in Washington, D.C. should be closed since there was nothing new left to discover. Megan approached her husband.

"Well, Duane, there may still be something left out there for us to discover. Maybe just something tiny... or..."

"Or something very big! Maybe even huge," Evan Nestor said. "And I still don't see why I can't pick my own story! I am big enough to read on my own, you know. I say we give the Smarty-Pants books to charity!"

"Yes, or something big," Megan continued. "But, starting with small things, we'll see what we can discover on our outing in the woods tomorrow."

"Honey, really," Duane scoffed. "I am a scientist. I have seen three generations of biology textbooks since I have been a teacher, and they have hardly changed from one to the next. Why? Because there is nothing left to find, nothing important left..."

"To discover? Well, maybe," Megan smiled. "Still, I think we might find something big. Really big. They just found a new kind of chimpanzee in Africa, didn't they? And a new kind of antelope in Asia. Those are big things. Who can say? In fact, Mr. I'm-So-Sure-of-Everything, I'll bet you five dollars that we *do* find something new! Five dollars, what do you think?" She winked at Evan Nestor.

"I'll take that bet!" Duane grinned at his wife, then his son, and sat down on the edge of the bed, picking up a tattered book from the floor.

"Okay, buddy-boy, now for another chapter from *Vernon the Gnome Explains Life Cycles of Molds and Fungi*."

Chapter 2

The little red ball, like many of the things Annette found at campsites after the campers left, was not made for an enormous Sasquatch hand. And everything about Annette was enormous. She was nearly twice as big as most of the campers: the hairless dads, moms, and children whom she knew were called Humans. They weren't the most attractive creatures, hairless as they were, and they had a terrible smell. But after years of watching them in the dark as they sat around their campfires, she felt affection for them.

In all that time of watching she had learned a lot. Of course, she and her kind, her people, had their own language, but she was learning the language the Humans spoke—or was trying to. There were words and phrases they said, like "ginormous," "monster truck," and "plus sizes," that she could not figure out. But she found she could make sense of many of their words and even say most of them herself, if not all.

Sasquatch life is a lonely life, unless you are part of a family, and Annette's last baby, Aidan Connor, was grown and off on his own. He had always wanted to go north to the Lake of the Great Orm, and he had done that years ago. Since then, Annette felt lonely quite often as she wandered around the misty, still forests by herself, and she had grown even more curious about the odd ways of the Humans. These creatures were like her own people in many interesting ways, but less predictable and reliable. She could not tell if they had what the Sasquatch called *mmnntum*, or gratitude and a sense of debt for any kindness done to them. If they lacked this, then they were truly dangerous and needed to be avoided, interesting though they were in other ways.

In addition, the Humans had become more curious about Annette and her people. Annette's mother was an impressive Sasquatch lady named Patty. One day, many years before Annette was born, Patty had been at Bluff Creek near the campsite, getting a sip of water and looking for mussels or frogs to munch on. Suddenly, two men on horseback appeared and took her picture. The smell of the horses had covered the smell of the men, and they had surprised her.

Annette had heard campers talking about this many times since then. It was all Annette and her people could do to stay hidden from the Humans who came to the woods to find them.

And Humans, who had to control and study everything, and were known to hunt every animal in the woods, had to be avoided. Her people knew that once the Humans, with their guns and ATVs, were sure that the Sasquatch were really there and not just a legend, it would be the end of them.

But Annette was fascinated by the Humans, threatening though they were. She marveled at their smallness, their machines, and how they put their food in fire before they ate it. How the men wore T-shirts that never covered their bellies and shorts that almost touched the ground. And that they were so undeniably hairless. What an awful burden, Annette thought: They must eat, sleep, and sit hairlessly, walk hairlessly, wash hairless babies in the stream, sleep hairlessly, and always pretend, when they are with their own kind, that the hairless thing in front of them is not ugly.

Humans were to be pitied, really. Pitied, and feared, unfortunately, because you never knew what they might do. Interesting and endearing as they sometimes were, yes, they had to be avoided. Annette's mother Patty could have been captured that day in the creek. If those men on horseback had decided to shoot her or tranquilize her, they could have done it. The Sasquatch had learned to live with the native people thousands of years ago, but the new people, the settlers with guns and machines, were different. The Sasquatch agreed many generations ago they could not let these new Humans get that close to them. They agreed that the survival of their way of life depended upon none of them, not one, ever being captured or photographed or shot by the new Humans. It was resolved by a council before, that the Sasquatch should never reveal themselves to these new beings. Patty had nearly broken that rule on that fateful day.

Patty's encounter had been an accident, her own carelessness. Annette worried that her curiosity about the Humans and her loneliness could be her undoing someday, and that all the Sasquatch people could suffer for it.

Finally, after many minutes of trying, Annette was able, with her stiff fingers and short thumb, to pick up the red ball and tiny metal stars the little girl had left at the campsite the day before. For a few minutes before the campers had left, she had watched the little girl picking up the metal stars from the ground while she bounced the red ball. Annette wondered if this was some sort of odd ritual, or if it was a kind of playing Human children did, like some of the games with pebbles and snails her own son had played when he was little. Annette would hide these odd objects in her secret rock overhang with the other Human treasures she saved and wondered over.

Chapter 3

When he was an eleven-year-old boy who accepted the fact that he liked ice cream cake and Splersh, the beet soda with a hint of cinnamon, a little too much, because as often as not they made him sick to his stomach, Wesley Interruptus Buttinski saw something he would never forget. He saw a film on the evening news that had been shot ten years earlier at Bluff Creek near his home. It showed a Sasquatch, plain as the cherry on top of a hot fudge sundae, walking across the creek and into the woods. The newsman said the whole thing was a mystery, or maybe a hoax, and he interviewed an odd person named Reynard, who said he was a retired modern dancer who had devoted his life to proving Sasquatch are real.

Reynard had founded a group called the Crypto Contempos, and he promised the newsman and all of Northern California that he and his group would accomplish their goal to give the world the evidence it needed that this species was real. The creature in that bit of film was no hoax, he said. Wesley could see that the Sasquatch was no hoax, and he could also see that Reynard was not the man to settle the question.

At that moment, Wesley knew instantly what his life's work must be: he could not allow anyone but himself to prove the existence of this hairy giant.

He went right out to the shed that very night and found an old bear trap his grandfather had owned. He baited it and set it in his front yard. His father immediately told him those traps were illegal now and to put it back where it belonged, and why wasn't he in bed yet since it was an hour past his bedtime? Wesley did as he was told, but when he went to bed that night, his mind was racing. There is more than one way to skin a cat, as the old saying goes, and that means there's more than one way to catch a Sasquatch.

Wesley knew his new ambition made his mother, Juanita, proud, because she had been interested in the subject all her life. Before she was married, Juanita was one of the Portland Muttermouths. "Remember son, you are a Portland Muttermouth," she always reminded him, often interrupting him or anyone else talking at the time to say it. They were a family know for gun collecting, baking, and never letting other people finish a sentence. And for cryptozoology, the search for unknown animals.

As a girl one Fourth of July, Juanita had found a new species of red squirrel in the Gifford Pinchot National Forest. As she had explained to Wesley, she felt she had the right to give the animal a scientific name, as its discoverer, but unfortunately, she had failed Latin in school. But she longed for something more. She wanted the big prize. She wanted the legendary Sasquatch, to be given to the world—especially the doubting, scientific world who knew Latin—by a Buttinski.

Now a grown man, Wesley carried on the work. He didn't really get along well with most other people and had even been considered something of a bully back in his school days, so the career suited him well. He lived alone in his old family house in the woods, snacking and nibbling on sweets more than he knew he should, sometimes just out of boredom.

Because none of his diets or exercise programs seemed to work, his knees were not what they used to be. He also had a habit of falling asleep suddenly at unfortunate times, so tramping through the woods was not his favorite thing.

But Wesley believed in technology. He fitted his house with radar, heat-sensing equipment, and cameras, both regular and night vision, and he surrounded his home with snare and pit traps. He figured he would make a Sasquatch come to him.

To bait the traps, Wesley decided that no food was more likely to attract the enormous creature than freshly baked cupcakes that had been deep fried. Wesley loved them, and he reasoned that his quarry would, too. Wesley spent much of his time baking the cupcakes, then frying them, taking a nap, then loading the cupcakes into his ATV and depositing them into the snare traps at the edge of his yard and up by the highway. Sometimes, twice this week in fact, he couldn't resist tasting the fried cupcakes as he put them down and got caught in his own snares.

"I should just leave them alone," he would say glumly to himself. "There's no reason these cupcakes wouldn't taste the same as the other ones I tried. I don't have to check every one!" But he was not often able to take his own advice.

Actually, at this very moment, Wesley was hanging upside down from a snare trap, munching on a fried cupcake and getting sleepy. His cell phone rang.

"Wesley, this is your..."

"...Hello, Mom," Wesley interrupted.

"Well, how are you, son..."

"...Hanging upside down again. How do you think I am?"

"Did you set off a trap aga—"

"Mom, Mom, of course," Wesley never considered it rude to interrupt a question he considered to be a stupid question.

"You need to leave those cupcakes alo—"

"Leave them alone after I catch a Sasquatch and

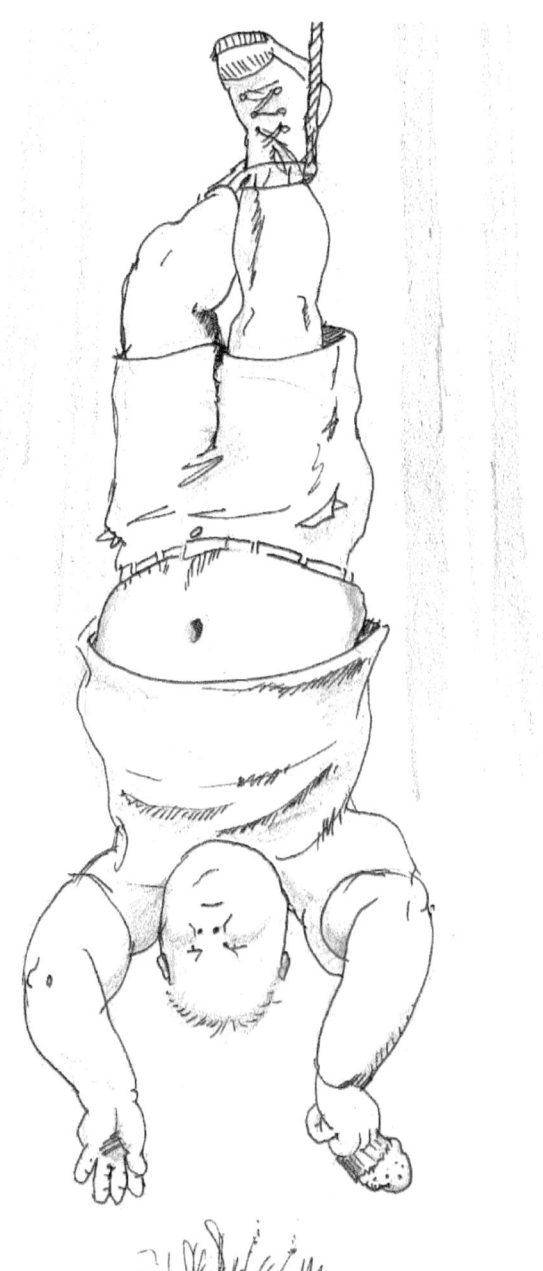

don't need to bait traps anymore. Big female around here and I'm closing in on her... Oops!" Wesley dropped the phone.

"Morning, Wesley." It was Jasper the mailman, stuffing Wesley's mailbox. "You been setting traps aga—"

"Jasper, Jasper. Looks that way, doesn't it?" Wesley butted in.

"Want me to cut you down this time, or—" Jasper began.

"Lower me down. And put my mail in the ATV," Wesley interrupted. "I'm getting sleepy."

"Okay." Jasper nodded. "Mailbox is only a hundred feet from your house," Jasper said, removing Wesley's mail from the box. "Why do you pick it up in the ATV?"

Wesley munched the last bite of his cupcake. "Because I believe in technology," he said.

Chapter 4

Duane, Megan and Evan Nestor stopped their bicycles at the top of a hill that was covered in ferns, moss and pine trees. The day was clear and warm and a little breeze that carried bird songs in it was blowing through the mountain passes and across the foothills. Evan Nestor spotted a tiny blue flower on the hillside near to where he stood with his bicycle. He picked it.

"What kind of flower is this, Dad?" he asked.

"Hmmmm." It took a moment for Duane to answer. He was very out of breath from pedaling his bike. "It looks like a pink checker bloom." Duane looked puzzled.

"But its blue, Dad. Could it be some other kind of flower? Something we've never seen before, maybe?"

Megan shrugged. "Must be," she said. Evan Nestor gave her the flower.

"No, not possible!" Duane frowned. "Blue or not, it must be a pink checker bloom."

"You never let me be right! You just don't want to lose your bet with Mom. Can we go now, Dad?"

"I think," Duane panted, "we need to give you a little more time to catch your breath. And I'm not worried about losing a bet. That's just... nonsense."

A strange cry floated through the forest. It almost sounded human.

Evan Nestor looked warily into the forest surrounding them. "What was that?" he said. He couldn't pinpoint exactly why, but the sound made him think of the night the Snow Monster came to life.

Duane shrugged. "Who can say, son? I don't know."

"Dad," Evan Nestor continued, "what kinds of animals live here?"

Duane sat on the ground. "Well, there are raccoons and possums and gray foxes and mule deer... and mountain lions."

"Anything else?"

"Oh, you might see a black bear now and then."

"Nothing bigger?" Evan Nestor untied Froggums from around his waist. He hugged the frog.

"No, nothing, son." Duane smiled. "You don't want anything bigger than a black bear, believe me. There are no monsters or giants, if that's what you're afraid of."

Evan Nestor blushed. "I bet you don't know everything," He mumbled. His dad didn't hear this.

Evan Nestor was hugging Froggums in an uncertain, frightened way. Megan laid her bicycle on the ground.

"Well, why don't we see what small things we can

find under these ferns and logs," she said, and smiled at Evan Nestor.

A cell phone rang. It was Duane's.

"Hello? Yes, hello, Reggie. What? Mr. Squirmy is loose? And Twitchy the hamster? Holy guacamole! A boa constrictor and a hamster both loose in the same classroom! That's a disaster in the making! But how did they get out? The custodian was racing them? Not again! Okay, I'll be right there."

"That doesn't sound good," Megan said.

Duane looked at her sternly. "If I don't find Twitchy before Mr. Squirmy does, that's another seven dollars from the biology budget right down the drain."

Evan Nestor was puzzled. "What do you mean, Dad?"

"Ummm, I mean... I have a hamster to save. Will you two be okay?"

"Sure," Megan said. "You go on. We'll be fine." She kissed Duane on the cheek.

He plopped himself onto his bicycle and pedaled away down the hill in the direction from which they had come. Megan waved after him.

Evan Nestor moved closer to the edge of the road to see how high a hill they were on.

"Mom," he said, "how come Dad has to be so right about everything? It seems like whatever I say, he says its wrong!"

Megan frowned a little. Evan Nestor noticed that she did this every time he asked her this question, which he had done many times before. She continued to watch Duane as he coasted further and further away from them. "That's a little bit of an exaggeration, isn't it?"

Evan Nestor shrugged.

"He doesn't mean to sound like that." Megan continued. "He was a very smart boy when we were in school. Kinda nerdy. Sometimes kids make fun of a kid like that, you know. Even… pick on them sometimes. I've always thought he needed to show everybody that being smart and bookish was a good thing, and maybe that makes it harder for him to admit he's wrong about anything."

Suddenly Megan's eyes widened, and she reached into her pocket. "Oh no! I have your dad's key ring! He'll need these to drive to the high school!"

She pulled out her cell phone and dialed him. After many rings, Megan saw Duane stop his bicycle in the distance and answer his phone.

"Hello," he said, still out of breath.

"I have your keys," she said. "Stop right there and we'll bring them to you."

"Okay," Duane agreed, "but hurry."

Megan closed her phone and put it away. "Back on your bike, Mister Bettancourt," she said, turning around. "We have to go."

But to her surprise, and panic, though his bicycle was still where he'd left it, Evan Nestor was nowhere to be seen.

Chapter 5

When Evan Nestor awoke, he was lying in a clump of ferns at the bottom of a hill. His head hurt and he felt a bump above his right ear. He held Froggums's hand in his own. He had just been dreaming that his mom and his dad were calling his name and that they had walked past him as he lay hidden in the ferns, but he had not been able to answer. And they eventually walked away. He sat up.

He saw broken ferns and footsteps in the soft ground close to him. It hadn't been a dream; his parents had been there searching for him. And he'd missed them.

"Mom?" he called. "Mom and Dad?" No answer.

Evan Nestor stood and felt very dizzy for a moment. He looked behind him at the steep hillside. He knew he could not climb such a steep slope to get back to the road. He would have to find an easier place to climb back up again.

He had been raised to love the forest. He and his parents spent many weekends hiking and camping, and it had always been his favorite thing that they did as a family. But he had never been in the woods completely alone before. Alone, everything seemed so different, more threatening and less friendly somehow.

Evan Nestor started to walk unsteadily along the

bottom edge of the hill in the direction he thought would take him back toward town. As he went along, the hillside next to him got steeper, and Evan Nestor found he had to go further and further down the hillside to keep moving in the same direction.

By the time Evan Nestor was starting to feel tired, and his legs were getting scratched by branches and twigs and rocks along the way, and he had been startled by a raccoon that scurried out from behind a rotting log, he was no longer sure that the hillside next to him was still the same one he had fallen down. He looked up the steep slope and saw thick stands of pine and spruce trees on the top of it, but nothing that looked like a road.

Evan Nestor heard all sorts of noises. He thought he heard something like a growl behind him, though it might have been the wind or a tree creaking. Bushes and ferns seemed to move and sway close to him, even though there was no breeze. He was certain he heard a branch breaking further down the hillside, and the woods were slowly getting darker. The sun was going down.

He clutched Froggums tightly. Should he keep walking in the direction he had been going, or should he try to go back to the spot where he had started? Why did he ever start walking in the first place? His parents had always told him that if he ever got lost in the woods, the best thing to do, if the area he was in was safe, is to just stay put and let people find him. He wished he had remembered this sooner instead of after he had been walking so long.

As he watched the tall, slowly swaying trunks become black in the dusk, he knew he was lost.

Chapter 6

Wesley's thermal-imaging screen sat right above the TV in his living room. One Thursday night, three weeks earlier, while he was watching Tackzilla, a new reality show about a renegade, no-nonsense upholstery shop, an orange form suddenly flickered across the thermal screen. Wesley thought it was a raccoon at first, but as he munched corn chips and sipped his Splersh, the image grew larger and more interesting. While he ate salsa and a crunchy chalupa, the image grew taller and more like a bear, but it was not a bear. As Wesley finished off a ham sandwich, a half bag of ripple chips, another bottle of Splersh, and two coconut cupcakes drizzled with caramel sauce which he couldn't quite resist though he tried, the image on the thermal screen finally revealed itself clearly and plainly, to Wesley's great excitement. It was *huge*; at least seven-and-a-half feet tall. It stood upright on two legs like a human, but it was not a human.

Wesley dropped his cruller. The creature on the imaging screen had a pointed head, small for its enormous body, long arms, thick legs, and big, big feet. And it was a female.

It was Sasquatch! No doubt about it!

Wesley moved slowly toward the kitchen to get

ketchup to put on the French fries he'd just microwaved, watching the figure of the Sasquatch the whole time. In another second, the creature stooped to pick up a fried cupcake from one of Wesley's snare traps that was very close to the road near Wesley's property.

Sproing!

Snap!

As the Sasquatch sprung the trap, the rope snare broke like a thread against the weight of the great beast. The creature munched a few more cupcakes, then disappeared into the dark forest.

Wesley knew he should have used a new rope on that trap, and he promised himself he would spare no expense and use new ropes from now on.

Three weeks later, after much planning and unplanning, packing and unpacking, Wesley was prepared to search for and find that Sasquatch. He had found her footprints around his traps in the last few days, and he'd made plaster impressions of them, tripped and broken the casts, and then tried to cast them again. His trail cameras mounted on tree trunks had snapped several fuzzy photographs, and stuck in tree bark and in his fence posts he had found and collected long strands of black hairs that he'd saved in plastic sandwich bags.

"The Scientific Method," Wesley's mother Juanita had told him when he was eleven, after he had announced to her his life's ambition, "must be used at all times if we are ever to prove that these creatures exist, and if we are to be taken seriously as researchers. You must always... umm... pay obeisance to the Scientific Method, for want of a better word. Obeisance. That's another word for your Words To Look Up List for this week. If it helps you remember, think of it as the... the... Scienterrific Method!"

"I will pay obesity to it!" Wesley agreed.

And now, after a lifetime of searching, he was ready to find this creature.

Wesley packed his compass, pocketknife, stun gun, night-vision goggles, camera, and a bag full of tuna fish sandwiches, red licorice, and Mallomars into his backpack and headed outside to his ATV. He yawned. He was ready to do something he had rarely done in his life: go out into the woods, away from the roads and trails, and search for Sasquatch.

Chapter 7

Megan and Duane looked anxiously across the desk at Sheriff Fletcher. The sheriff was a middle-aged man who looked uncomfortable in his sheriff's uniform. The buttons down the front of his shirt were under a great deal of pressure from his stomach beneath them, and they appeared as though they might fly across the desk at any moment. His belly was splotched with stains that looked like coffee in some places and in others like ketchup or mustard. He wore wire-rimmed glasses on the tip of his nose and a sort of bathing cap of aluminum foil on his head.

Over his left shoulder, thumbtacked to the wall just under a large county map, was a poster with a flying saucer on it with a caption that read I WANT TO BELIEVE. Someone had taken a black marker and crossed out "Want" and written in "Do."

I Do To Believe? Megan thought. *What sense does that make?*

"It's the secret epidemic nobody wants to talk about!" the sheriff said. "It happened to me right in this office, and it's happening to millions of people around the world. It wouldn't be fair to you as concerned parents to not consider the possibility. I'm talking, of course, about alien abduction."

Duane had heard enough. "Sheriff Fletcher! We don't believe in any of that! Our son tumbled down a hill. He is lost in the woods, not a captive on a UFO."

"Not saying he is," Fletcher said. "Hoping he isn't, I'm just saying, don't rule it out. Exa-tressials are real. They want us to not believe in them. They like non-believers. They made me believe, though. Grabbed me! It happened to me right in this office!"

"Now Eugene," Doris the police dispatcher said as she walked past Fletcher's desk on her way to the break room. "You fell asleep in that very chair. It was Super Bowl weekend, so there were no calls coming in. You were asleep in that chair the whole time. I saw you!"

"I know what happened, Doris," Fletcher said curtly. "Thank you."

"He is lost, frightened and alone," Megan said. "He is a frightened little boy anyway..."

"Monsters, and... and... giants." Duane put in. "Fascinated by them and afraid of them."

"Deputy Clark's team is on the scene right now, we have dogs coming, and Search and Rescue will be there in minutes. Department of the Interior. The best," Fletcher said. "You can come with me out there if you'd like, but I really feel you'd be better off at home. Just wait to hear from us."

Duane and Megan looked at each other.

"We want to come with you," Megan said. "We want to be there when he's found. We want to be the first thing he sees."

Fletcher looked at them seriously. "Well, I understand. If he was my little boy, I would do exactly the same thing. Yes, I would. So... will you be wanting aluminum foil for your heads? I recommend it."

"Huh?" Duane was puzzled.

"Everybody knows they—" Fletcher nodded skyward— "the exa-tressials, can read your thoughts unless you block them with foil. It's common knowledge. TV and movies make fun of it, make people who cover their heads look crazy, but making a joke out of it doesn't mean it isn't true. Their tuknology is that advanced. I'm just trying to make my job easier."

Duane and Megan looked at each other again.

"No, Sheriff. I don't think we will," Duane said.

Fletcher shrugged and opened his desk drawer. He rummaged around for a few seconds, then withdrew a large plastic bag and handed it to Megan.

"If you please, Mrs. Bettancourt," he said. "This is for any devices or implants you find on the boy after he's recovered. There are people, including myself, who would find them very useful and informative. If we can figure out their tuknology, we can stay a step ahead of them. Now," he said as he rose from his desk chair, "I think we should join Deputy Clark."

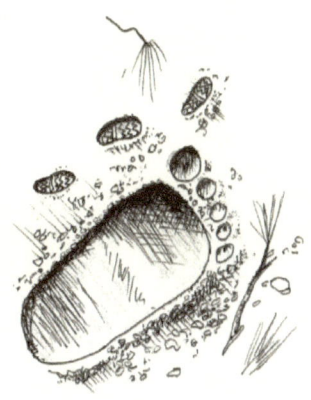

Chapter 8

When Evan Nestor opened his eyes, for a moment, he couldn't remember where he was.

Damp, moss-covered rocks hung over him, and he was shivering. His clothes, his hair and skin felt damp, too, and his fingers and the tip of his nose hurt from the cold.

He could see that the sun was out, and it was a bright and sunny day. He noticed the sounds of birds singing, which he hadn't noticed since yesterday, and a little breeze was stirring through the valley.

He remembered he was lost.

"Mom and Dad?" he said quietly. No answer. "Mom and Dad?" More loudly this time, but still no answer.

He felt the fear pain in his stomach that he sometimes felt when he thought he heard a monster in his closet or outside his window at night. He thought he might cry, but he really didn't want to, even though there was no one there to see him and make him feel embarrassed.

He crawled a little closer to the edge of the shadowy rock overhang that was protecting him. It was on a steep hillside, and he was overlooking a small valley filled with pine and spruce trees, covered by a carpet of ferns.

The ground was loose, rich-smelling dirt, and it felt

almost like a soft cushion to Evan Nestor. As he crawled forward, his hand touched something hard in the soil. His fingers closed around the object. It was gold in color and light, like plastic. Evan Nestor looked at it. It was a tube of lipstick, like he had seen on his mother's makeup tray in the bathroom. He smiled, feeling comforted.

Evan Nestor suddenly remembered Froggums. He was relieved to find the frog on the ground behind him. The still-shivering boy picked up the drooping, dirty toy and looked at it respectfully. He was glad he had not lost his frog, and glad he had decided he had not outgrown Froggums just yet.

Evan Nestor put the lipstick back on the ground. He ran his fingers through the dirt again. He felt another object, but larger than the lipstick. He pulled out of the dirt a pink hand mirror with blue flowers painted on it. There was a little crack in the glass at the bottom edge, but otherwise the mirror was in good condition for being buried in the ground.

A lipstick. A hand mirror. These were things that belonged not to a kid or a dad, but to a mom. Evan Nestor's own mom had things like this. She had her share of bicycling equipment and skiing equipment, and even woodworking tools, for she was better at fixing things than Dad was. Still, mirrors and lipsticks were mom things. Evan Nestor wondered how these mom things had come to be here. He smiled again as he puzzled over the mystery.

He looked above himself along the rock wall. There was a sort of shelf in the stone above him, and he could see something long and white sticking out beyond the edge of the shelf.

Evan Nestor stood to look closer. The object was a hairbrush. And there were many other things on the rock shelf, too. There was a plastic dinosaur, a ball and jacks, a pocketknife, an adjustable wrench and screwdriver, a coupon for one dollar off a fish plate at Ahab's Fish and Chips, and a Decepto-Bot action figure from the planet Mendacitron 4.

Evan Nestor was amazed that all these things had been collected together out in the woods. Who could have done it? He picked up the Decepto-Bot and sat on the ground to think.

"I don't know who left this here," he whispered to himself, "but it's mine now, and Dad can't give this away either!"

A rustle of twigs on the ground down the hillside startled Evan Nestor. He slowly crept on his hands and knees backward and further into the rock overhang. In a few moments, he saw a little gray mound of fur pop up above the lower edge of the rock opening. Some animal was creeping up the hillside. Suddenly, two pointed ears could be seen, then a shiny black snout. It was a gray fox. The fox stopped abruptly when it saw Evan Nestor back in the shadows.

Evan Nestor smiled, not knowing if he should be afraid or not. The fox's ears quickly pricked up and it looked first to its left, then to its right. In a moment, Evan Nestor realized he could hear what the fox was hearing: a very low and steady growl. He hugged Froggums tightly.

In an instant, the fox seemed to see something that startled it, and it ran off. The low, growling sound continued and grew louder. Instead of a furry gray mound at the rim of the overhang, Evan Nestor now saw a dull, yellow one. The mound grew into a muscular back, a strong neck and a wide, round head set with terrible, yellow eyes.

It was a mountain lion!

A stab of fear shot through Evan Nestor's stomach. There were tears in his eyes, and he wanted to close them, but he could not. The lion's eyes looked deeply into Evan Nestor's, and he found he could not look away. The animal crept closer to the overhang.

Then, suddenly from somewhere above, an arm reached down and grabbed the lion by the skin of its shoulders, as if it were a kitten. It was an arm like no arm Evan Nestor had ever seen before: it was huge and covered with long, black hair, and its wrist and forearm were as big around as one of his dad's legs, at least.

The great cat rose off the ground with a puzzled expression on its face. In another second, it was tossed down the hillside with an indignant hiss, and Evan Nestor heard it crash into some brush somewhere far below. He heard an indignant snarl and the sound of the lion running off through the underbrush. There was no other sound for many minutes, and Evan Nestor did not move. Whatever had saved him must have gone. Slowly and very quietly, he crawled toward the front of the overhang.

As Evan Nestor neared the front of the overhang, he saw something just to the right of the opening. It looked like the edge of a huge foot standing still on the moss. It looked like a person's foot, but so much bigger that Evan Nestor could hardly imagine it. And it was covered with long, black hair.

The foot didn't move.

Evan Nestor crept out a little further.

His fear filled his stomach and head, but his curiosity was strong.

Could this be a monster? Could this be a nice monster who had deliberately saved him?

The enormous foot was attached to a thick leg the size of a tree trunk, bulging with muscles, and covered in hair. The creature still did not move, but stood facing away from Evan Nestor, as if it were looking down the hillside where it had tossed the mountain lion.

Finally, Evan Nestor poked his whole head out from under the rock overhang and saw the entire great creature standing there so very close to him. It was a giant, like the Snow Monster come to life in his room that night, but even bigger, and without a doubt, real.

"I knew I didn't imagine it!" he gasped to himself. "This must be what I saw that night, I... think!" Now no one could tell him this creature wasn't real. At least, no one could if there was anyone else there to see it too.

It was taller than the top of Mom's head when she

sits on Dad's shoulders in the Neptune's Envy aboveground swimming pool in the summer. Taller than the gutters on their house. It was a mountain of muscle and black hair. Its arms hung low, nearly to its knees, and its back was wider than Evan Nestor's mattress. A true giant.

Evan Nestor gasped when he realized the creature was slowly turning toward him. He had no place to run. Before he could move, the great face was looking at him. Its mouth was wide and thin-lipped and opened a little, showing several white, flat teeth. The eyebrow ridges were heavy like a gorilla's, and the top of its head was pointed. And sitting on the broad, flat nose was a pair of heart-shaped, bright pink sunglasses.

Chapter 9

Evan Nestor was frozen with fear. He knew he couldn't move or run away. And even if he tried, his legs were trembling so violently that he couldn't have gotten far.

The hairy giant didn't move either. She looked down on him for many moments through the pink, heart-shaped sunglasses that Evan Nestor now noticed didn't fit her very well, but did make her somehow less terrifying. At length, she slowly reached up and removed the sunglasses. Her eyes were as black as the deepest corner of Evan Nestor's closet on the darkest night. And they were locked on him.

The giant slowly turned around so she faced the boy.

"Are you... a monster?" Evan Nestor's voice was weak and quivering.

The giant frowned a bit and opened her mouth. She made a low, odd sound.

"Mmm... mmm... st... rrr."

"Monster?" Evan Nestor repeated.

"Mmmsstrrr," Annette the giant repeated. "Mmmssttrrr... no..." she grunted.

Evan Nestor could not believe what he had just heard. He had not asked his question really expecting an answer. It had just sort of popped out of him. But he had been answered! This huge creature—it must be a Sasquatch like he had seen on TV—had spoken to him! He stared at the giant in wonder and fear for many moments.

"Holy guacamole," he mumbled to himself, "Dad really, really lost his bet!"

Annette showed her teeth at Evan Nestor. Some of the fear left when he recognized that what she was doing with her mouth was a smile. Annette extended her arm toward him and bent over. Evan Nestor did not move. She held her huge hand, palm up, short fingers curled, in front of him.

"Mmmnnn," she said. For a moment Evan Nestor was puzzled. Then he understood. He placed the Decepto-Bot action figure in the enormous hand. Annette placed the toy on the rock ledge with her other treasures.

"Sorry," Evan Nestor said. "I was just looking at it."

He wondered if this giant knew any human words, maybe from hearing them around campfires at night, or listening to hikers, and he wondered if she ever practiced speaking them. He wondered also, because of the way she pronounced "mine," if there were some words, and parts of words, which she could not say.

"I am Evan Nestor," he continued. "Evan."

Annette frowned.

"Rrrr," she said, "...rrrrvnnn."

"Yes...Evan," he smiled.

"Rrrvnnn," she repeated.

"Do you have a name?"

"Nnnmmm...nmmm," she struggled to form the words, "...nnn...uunnnuutt. Unnutt."

"Alphabet? Internet?... Annette?" Evan Nestor asked.

She smiled a little.

"Annette!" Evan Nestor repeated. "Annette! And I'm Evan Nestor!" He stood. He was barely taller than her knee. "And I'm lost."

"Lssssst," Annette nodded. She recognized the word. "Lssst." She waved her shaggy tree-trunk arm away from herself.

"Yes, lost." Evan Nestor could tell she understood. "I was with my mom and dad, and I'm lost."

Annette seemed to nod in understanding. She flattened her right hand against her chest.

"Mmmmm," she said. "Mmm…"

"You mean 'me?'" Evan Nestor asked. "Mom… me?"

Annette nodded.

"Uh… uh… uhdnn. Uhhdnn Cnnnr," she said.

"Uhhh, Unmasked Condor? Undone Conman? Aidan Connor?" Evan Nestor said with a puzzled frown. He had friends with both of those names. They weren't as smart as he was, but they were still his friends. "Is that your boy's name?"

Annette nodded again and smiled a little. Again, she made the away gesture.

"He's gone." Evan Nestor understood.

Annette nodded.

"Funny names you got… for a Sasquatch," Evan Nestor said, although he couldn't really say what normal names would be. "Guess you heard them from people, people you listened to in the woods?"

Annette nodded at him and sat down on the soft ground with something of a thud. Evan Nestor sat down next to her. He looked at her cautiously but with fascination. He could scarcely believe that this had happened, and that this huge being next to him was real. She seemed to be a little out of breath, and he noticed that among her shaggy black hairs were many white ones.

His stomach growled a little. Annette turned away from him and broke off some branches of a heavily laden blueberry bush. She handed the branches to Evan Nestor.

"You protected me," Evan Nestor said. "You saved me from the mountain lion. He would have eaten me. You don't share your things very well, though. My dad says I don't share very well, either. But neither do you." He began to munch on the delicious, sweet berries. "You're not a monster," he said, juice running down his chin. "And you're not my imagination. You're a mom."

Chapter 10

Evan Nestor was doing his best to keep up with Annette. She was leading them down a steep hillside in a direction that, it seemed to Evan Nestor, who had never been more lost in his life, was going away from the road. "Where are we going?" Evan Nestor called. Annette grunted and made a slight waving motion as if she wanted him to keep up with her better. Her back was like a hillside itself. The muscles of her sloping shoulders were an enormous triangle of flesh, easily as wide as Evan Nestor was tall. Wider, in fact.

The hillside they walked on was covered with ferns and rocks and pine needles that were all very damp and slippery. Evan Nestor slipped and made the side of his leg muddy. He got up and slipped again. "You have to slow down!" He said angrily. "I can't keep up! It's rude for you to go so fast."

Annette stopped and turned. She looked at Evan Nestor for a moment. He looked back at her warily. He couldn't tell if she was angry or not. "You have to think about the other person," he continued meekly. "Like mom says. I can't keep up if you go so fast."

After another moment, Annette nodded.

"Sllwwwrrr," she said. She held her arm out toward him and pointed a huge finger. In a moment he realized what she wanted him to do. He grabbed her finger with his hand, though his whole hand would barely fit around it, and they started to walk again.

They continued down the slope more slowly and carefully. The ground was wet enough to muffle the sounds of their walking, so when a twig snapped in the forest somewhere behind them, they could easily hear it. Annette stopped and looked back. Evan Nestor could hear a slight huffing sound and what seemed to be a little growl. He could tell that Annette heard it too. She frowned, and they continued their slow way downward.

Evan Nestor could see a wide valley through the trees below them. At first, he thought it was a meadow, but he could soon see that it was not a natural meadow. There were tree stumps across the valley, hundreds of stumps of trees that had been cut down. It was an old logging camp: one that looked as though it had not been used for many years. At the far edge of the camp, against the tree line, stood a dilapidated white trailer with a very old, rusted pickup truck parked in front of it. There was an ancient bulldozer beyond the trailer that had saplings growing up around it, some old flatbed trailers, and a rusted yellow and black crane with a few loads of rotting logs still wrapped in rusted chains scattered next to it. This camp had not been used for more years than he had been alive, Evan Nestor thought.

They entered the clearing, and to Evan Nestor's surprise, they headed right for the old trailer.

"We're going there?" he whispered to himself.

There were power lines connected to the trailer and a television dish on the top. It looked as though someone was still living there. When they were about a hundred feet from the trailer, its front door flew open. A very grizzled and unkempt old man with a scruffy beard and dressed only in dirty long underwear stood in the doorway. Evan Nestor looked up at Annette. Surely she did not want to be seen by this human.

"Annette! Annette ye crazy fool! What are ye doin' out in the open in the daytime? Ye got more sense than that!"

Annette raised her hand in greeting to the old man.

"And what are ye bringin' a kid here for? A human kid?" the old fellow went on. "I got nothin' here for a kid. Not after yours et me outta house an' home!" The old man stopped for a moment, as if he just understood what he was looking at. "Where'd ye... wher'd ye get the kid?"

"Hmmm lsssstt," Annette said.

"Lost?" the old man repeated. "So what are ye

bringin' him here for? Kid, I don't know why she's bringin' ye here. I got nothin' for ye."

"I dunno," Evan Nestor shrugged. "Maybe you could call somebody to come and get me. Or take me home."

The old man threw his arms up in protest. "Gas costs money! I'm not a taxi service! I can't drive every kid a Sasquatch finds in the woods back home!"

"You mean this happened before?" Evan Nestor said. By now he and Annette had reached the trailer door. Annette was nearly as tall as the roof of the trailer.

"No, never!" the old man snapped. "What a silly question. And my phone doesn't work. Tower got hit by lightning. No signal. I got parts for the shortwave radio coming in a week. Ye can't stay here a week!"

Evan Nestor looked up at Annette. Was she really going to leave him with this horrible old man?

The old fellow suddenly calmed down a little and he asked, "What's yer name, kid?"

"Evan Nestor Bettancourt. I live in Krantz's Grove."

"Bettancourt, Bettancourt. I think I heard that name before. Ye have a grampa named Tancred Cuchulain Bettancourt?"

"Yeah. He died when I was little."

"I loaned him four dollars in 1952, and he never paid me back. Don't suppose ye got it, do ye?"

"No."

"Didn't think so. I'm Liam Bradley de la Courvoisier. Caretaker here. Worked for Ajax Lumber for forty-eight years. They let me keep livin' here when they left. I keep an eye on the equipment.

"And you, missy," Liam looked at Annette, "no apples for you! Yer boy et twenty of them when he was here last. All I had. I usually give ye five, so if ye come here three more times and I don't give ye any apples, then we'll be even!"

Annette shrugged. She touched the top of Evan Nestor's head.

"Tkkk Rrrrvvnn hmmm?" she asked.

Liam looked at Evan Nestor.

"Guess I'll get him to his people somehow," he said.

Annette smiled and looked down at Evan Nestor. She touched the top of his head again and patted Froggums. She made the away sign with her big right arm, then turned and started walking back toward the mountain from which they had come.

"Might as well come inside," Liam said and turned, disappearing back into the trailer. "I'm watching *Tackzilla*, and no, you can't change the channel!"

The inside of the trailer was very dark and very, very dirty. There were old newspapers and hunting magazines in piles everywhere, and dirty clothes and half-eaten food on chairs and countertops. The floor seemed to slope down toward an old television set, and a small dinette table was scattered with candy bars, potato chip crumbs, apple cores, and dirty dishes. Bugs skittered from one scrap of food or dirty dish to another.

"Don't expect anything fancy," Liam said. "I don't get fancy for people, and I didn't ask Annette to bring ye here. And stay away from my candy. It's mine, not yers!"

"You don't share very well," Evan Nestor mumbled.

"Huh? Couldn't hear ye. Ye need to speak up."

"You are friends with Annette?"

"Yup. Friends. Good friends. After the camp was abandoned, it took another few weeks, then I started to see the Sasquatch. Annette and Aidan Connor were the first, then some others. A family. Them talkin' their gibberish. They can learn our language, but can't talk it too well. Trouble saying vowels." Liam sat himself down in an old easy chair piled with clothes. "They were the skookum and wendigo. The mountain giants to the Indians. The earth giants of old, maybe. I don't know. They're company for me. All I want. I don't like visitors. But people are starting to look for them now. I see it on TV. Taking them seriously. That will be the end of them. Long as people don't believe in them, they're safe."

Evan Nestor wanted to sit down, but he wasn't sure where. He was a little thirsty, but imagined there wasn't a clean glass in the trailer.

"I'm... thirsty," he said.

"You see the faucet. Help yerself. I don't wait on people, and don't expect them to wait on me." Liam waved vaguely toward the kitchenette. "Oh," he said suddenly. "I took some pictures of Aidan Connor... and Annette ye might like to see. Secretly, 'cause they don't like it when you take their picture." Liam got up quickly from his chair and disappeared into a back room. "I been taking pictures of them secretly for years," he continued. "The Knowledge Channel would pay a lot for them, but I ain't sellin'. Don't ye touch any of my stuff while I'm in here!"

Evan Nestor noticed a half-eaten Mr. Crazydude bar on the dinette table. He thought for a second about taking a bite himself, from the unwrapped end, but just then a fat cockroach appeared from under the candy bar and crawled over its top. Evan Nestor had had enough. He could see Annette out the open door still making her way up the hillside. If he ran hard, in a few minutes he could catch up to her.

Chapter 11

Wesley was always proud to repeat the story of his ancestor Major Marcus Interruptus Buttinski and his service to the Union Army under General Atherton at the battle of Pike Ridge in 1863. What Juanita, Wesley's mother, had never told him was that when General Atherton tried to issue orders to his army to advance, Marcus interrupted him with a story about how a judge who had fined him for public rudeness didn't understand the law, and that interruption distracted the general and caused the battle to be lost. Never knowing this part of the story, Wesley had always thought of his ancestor as a hero and an example of determination and stick-to-it-iveness. Wesley felt he had that same determination in his search for Sasquatch.

And he was showing determination. He had been out in the woods for an hour. Well, actually, it would be an hour in fifteen more minutes. His food was nearly gone, and he had trekked almost two miles from home, but still he was not ready to turn back. Not yet. Not that he hadn't thought about it, but no, not yet. Wesley figured he could go ten minutes, maybe twenty, after he finished his last Malomar. That would be pushing the limit of his survival skills and endurance.

But Wesley had a trick up his sleeve. In the last batch of bait cupcakes he'd baked, which had all been eaten by the female Sasquatch, Wesley had hidden a tiny, electronic homing device. If he could manage to get in range of the signal, he could find the animal pretty quickly.

But right now, he was stuck in the mud. He had driven his ATV near the edge of a bog, and when he realized with a start that his food was all but gone, he had absentmindedly driven right into a mossy and muddy patch. As he sat wondering how long he could last without food, he removed a Mr. Crazydude candy bar from his vest pocket and took a bite. He was in a bit of a fix and needed to think.

His phone rang.

"Wesley? This is your mother…"

"I know, Mom. I have caller ID."

"How are y—"

"I'm stuck in the mud, Mom. How do you think I am?"

"How did you—"

"I'm out looking for the Sasquatch."

"Out?" Juanita sounded surprised.

"Out. She swallowed a homing device and I'm trying to pick up a signal."

"You're out in the woods?"

"Mom, Mom, how else can I track a wild animal?"

"Wesley! I am so proud of you! You are out in the world doing something!"

"And stuck in the mud and out of food." He removed a package of peanut butter crackers from another vest pocket. He tore open the package and ate one. "I'm probably going to starve!"

"Can't you just walk home?"

"Its two miles, Mom."

"Do you see any berries or dandelions or goldenrod nearby?"

"Uh, Mom… are they gluten free?"

"Yes. That is, I think so…"

"*Not interested!*" His phone clicked. "Mom, gotta go. Another call coming in."

Wesley pressed a button.

"Hello?"

"Wesley, it's Deputy—"

"…Clark, yeah."

"Yes, Deputy Clark. Since you're out that way, I wanted to let you know we have a lost little boy last seen three miles from your cabin—"

"Uh, Deputy, the pioneers lived in cabins, I live in a house," Wesley said sarcastically.

"All right, Wesley, your house then," Deputy Clark said patiently. "Search and Rescue are in the area, and the sheriff is on his way."

"The sheriff?" Wesley asked. "Isn't he afraid of being sucked up into a UFO if he goes out in the open?" He smiled.

"Yes... frankly, he is."

A glowing green glob suddenly flickered onto Wesley's tracking screen, followed by a beep. He had picked up the tracking signal.

"I'll be on the lookout for the little fellow, Deputy. I'm out in the woods now. I'll be in touch."

Wesley hung up his phone and turned on his thermal tracker. The orange blob appeared immediately on the screen: a huge, moving form walking upright through the woods about a half-mile away. And behind the huge form, now also clearly visible, the tiny shape of what appeared to be a little boy. Wesley smiled.

"You found each other," he said quietly. "And now I alone will find the both of you. My name will be even more well-known than Marcus Interruptus Buttinski's. Finally... I've got you."

Chapter 12

Sheriff Fletcher watched the sky nervously. Suspiciously. He flinched every time a bird flew overhead, or a leaf blew across the sky. Megan and Duane could see the sheriff was every bit as frightened of UFOs and the possibility of alien abduction as Evan Nestor was of the monsters he imagined were hiding in his closet or under his bed.

"Mr. and Mrs. Bettancourt," Fletcher said, "please don't worry. We'll find the little fellow."

"Thank you, Sheriff," Megan said, "We know you don't like to be out in the open like this."

"I have a job to do. A little boy has been abduct—" The sheriff stopped himself. "Is missing. Lost. And it is my duty to find him, and we will find him. Abductees are almost always returned! That's because the exa-tressials..."

Megan groaned and looked at Duane.

"Oh!" The sheriff realized what he had said. "Sorry, folks."

"It's okay, Sheriff," Duane interrupted. "Let's just find him."

"And find him we will," Fletcher nodded. "Search and Rescue will have bloodhounds here in twenty minutes to cover territory north and east of here. Deputy Clark's team will be south and west, and the

Krantz's Grove UFO Taskforce will be making sure nobody else misses anything."

Deputy Clark approached quickly from the road.

"We're heading out now, Sheriff," Clark said. "I called Wesley Buttinski and he's out too, looking over toward Bluff Creek."

The sheriff looked surprised.

"Wesley Interruptus Buttinski is out? You mean out of his cabin? Searching?"

"Yes, he is."

"He's not searching through ESP or remote viewing? He is physically out... in the woods?"

"Yes, Sheriff."

Duane looked at his wife. "We knew Wesley in school. Unless he's changed an awful lot, I don't think he's likely to help us."

"Please, can we get started?" Megan interrupted.

"We are started, Mrs. Bettancourt," Deputy Clark said. "Things are moving along."

"Yes," the sheriff agreed. "We'll join the deputy's party."

The sun was just coming up over the pines and spruces. Small ground squirrels were skittering about, looking for seeds and pine nuts.

Megan and Duane had the same thought at the same time. They looked at each other the way adults do when they think of something together. "Evan Nestor has just spent a night alone in the forest," Duane said. "He must be freezing... and terrified."

"We've talked to him about sheltering against rocks and boulders, and covering with pine needles and brush," Megan put in. "We have talked about that many times."

"We got such a late start yesterday," Duane said. "We looked for him for an hour before we came to you,

Sheriff. We should have called sooner, but I couldn't imagine we wouldn't find him quickly."

"I'm sure he's fine," Sheriff Fletcher said. "I'm sure he's okay."

"I know there are bear in these woods," Duane said anxiously, "and mountain lions."

"They're very rare, folks," Clark said. "And, of course, don't forget we're in Bigfoot country."

Duane scowled. "I've lived here all my life, Deputy Clark, and I've never seen one. There is no such thing. We're not looking for UFOs, and we're not looking for Bigfoot. We're just looking for a lost little boy!"

Megan gave her husband a little hug.

"Excuse me for saying it, Mr. Bettancourt," Sheriff Fletcher said after a moment, "but the Bigfoot are real, and it would be a stroke of luck, if you want to know the truth, if one of them did find your boy. They've been known to help people who are hurt or lost in the woods, save them from freezing and starvation. Yes, they're real. I've seen them myself—twice."

Deputy Clark looked stunned. "Sheriff, you never told me that..."

"Once when I was twelve and again when I was nineteen. While I was camping with my dad."

"But why didn't you ever mention it before?" Clark asked.

The sheriff looked at Deputy Clark with mild exasperation. "Because what in the world does Bigfoot have to do with UFOs?"

Chapter 13

Evan Nestor sat on a mossy pine log. His stomach still hurt. He had eaten all the berries and pine nuts, even a couple of fat grub worms Annette had brought him, and now he wasn't hungry anymore, but he didn't feel so well. The shallow river rushed by a few feet from him, where just minutes before Annette had been wading, trying to catch a trout among the submerged boulders. But Evan Nestor had told her that he was no longer hungry, that his stomach hurt. Annette understood, and she motioned for him to sit on the log. She then made the away gesture and climbed up the far bank and into the forest.

She had only been gone a few minutes, but already Evan Nestor was missing her and wondering if she would come back. She wouldn't feed him and protect him only to leave him alone in the woods, would she?

Just then, he heard movement on the mountainside where Annette had vanished, and he could see her making her way down the slope toward the riverbank.

As he watched her, Evan Nestor heard another sound, a sound he had heard before; the low growl he'd heard under the rock overhang that morning, and near Liam's trailer. It was coming from the hillside behind him. He turned and looked, but saw nothing.

In a moment, Annette was in the river again, wading toward him. In her hand she had several long, slender leaves. Evan Nestor smiled, stood up, and ran toward her.

"I was scared you wouldn't come back," he said.

Annette smiled a little. "Kmmmm bkkkk," she said. She crouched down on the blue, gray, and pink pebbles of the bank next to Evan Nestor. She handed him several long leaves. "Chwwuuu, chwwuuu," she said.

"Chew?" he asked. She nodded. He took the leaves and put them in his mouth. They had a slightly bitter taste, like a bug that had flown in there once, but not too bad. And soon he noticed that his stomach wasn't bothering him anymore.

"Hmmm," he said, "I feel better."

Annette nodded. Evan Nestor noticed that she was out of breath and seemed tired. She looked toward the hillside behind them.

"W... w... wuhh..."she started to say.

"We?" Evan Nestor asked. It was starting to get easier to understand what she was trying to say.

Annette nodded. "Crrrfflll. Lnnn flllwwwwnng sss."

"The lion is following us? The lion that wanted to eat me? I knew I heard it. I knew I didn't imagine it!"

Annette nodded again.

Evan Nestor turned to look at the hillside again, but still saw nothing. He felt the stab of fear and wished that his mom and dad were here to protect him. He thought he saw shapes moving in the bushes that must be the mountain lion, or maybe many mountain lions, all watching for their chance to grab him. Or was he imagining it?

Annette was watching the hillside, too, and though she was still a little out of breath, she looked carefully and closely into the woods as if she were ready for anything.

Evan Nestor watched the expression on her face for a few moments, then relaxed a little. He knew that as long as he stayed in the woods with Annette, he would be safe.

As they had made their way to the river earlier in the day, Annette had lifted Evan Nestor onto her shoulders when she had seen again that he could not keep up with her as they crossed the rough hillsides. Her neck was so thick he found it hard to hang on, but by leaning himself forward and wrapping his arms around the large crest on her head, he learned to manage it pretty well.

Now she held out her enormous hand and Evan Nestor took it. With a small twitch, she plopped him once again onto her shoulders.

"Where are we going?" he asked.

"Mmmmkkk nssst frrr nnnhhtt."

"Make a nest for the night."

"Hmmmmm."

Annette headed back along the riverbed, retracing their steps. Evan Nestor thought about his mom and dad, about how worried they must be. He was worried too, that they would worry too much about him, and be too sad. Because for all that he missed them, he knew they must miss him twice as much. They must miss making him snacks and buying him things and reading to him at bedtime. He hoped they were all right.

In fact, he realized that he was more worried about them than he was for himself. Kind of an odd thing to feel, he thought. As for himself, now he was not afraid. If the lion was following them, or there were bears out there, or bobcats, or any real monsters that Evan Nestor had not yet even imagined, he knew there was nothing bigger or stronger in the woods than Annette, and knew she would let nothing out here hurt him.

At a sharp bend in the river, where many pine logs and branches had collected on the rocks, Annette climbed up the bank and into the forest. Not far up the hillside there was a pine tree that had fallen against a spruce tree, and the one trunk against the other formed a triangle shape.

"Nnssstt hrrrrr," Annette said, and she carefully placed Evan Nestor on the ground. She pulled a birch sapling out of the ground and twisted it around the trunk that had fallen against the pine tree, along with some spruce saplings behind it. She layered tree bark and moss onto the structure she was creating. After just a few minutes, she had formed a shallow, cave-like shelter. Then she covered the top with pine boughs and branches. Evan Nestor was amazed at how easily Annette snapped the trunks of the saplings, some as thick as the baseball bat he'd gotten on Bat Day when his family had gone to San Francisco to see the Giants play last summer.

The sun was well below the hillsides now, and the rushing sound of the river seemed softer and more muted, quiet enough that the burring of the tree frogs could be heard as evening settled into the valley. Evan Nestor was tired, and he wished (and this was the first time he ever remembered wishing it) that he could brush his teeth.

Annette sat on the ground, which was scattered with pinecones. Evan Nestor sat in front of her squeezing Froggums. He looked at her for a few moments as if he expected her to say something, or to announce to him the next thing they should do. Annette smiled at him.

"When your boy was little... Aidan Connor... what kind of things did you do with him? Did you play with him?" Evan Nestor said.

"Plllddd," Annette said, and she nodded. She looked around her on the ground until she found a particularly long, thin pinecone.

"Mmmkkk wwwrrrrmmm," she said.

"Make a worm?" Evan Nestor was very puzzled.

Annette enclosed the pinecone in her left hand so that the top of it was not visible in her fist, but most of it hung down below. She slowly started to squeeze the pinecone gently and repeatedly until it began to climb up through Annette's fist like a living, enormous caterpillar. Then, placing her right fist on top of her left and continuing the motion, she made it appear that the huge caterpillar was continuously climbing upwards.

"That looks alive!" Evan Nestor shouted. "Do it again!"

Annette repeated the trick again and again until the pinecone crumbled away.

Evan Nestor thought he should do something special for Annette.

"Hold this for just a minute," he said, giving Froggums to her. He ran up the riverbank a short way to where a clump of goldenrod was growing. Evan Nestor knew how his own mom, and other moms, as far as he could tell, liked to have flowers picked for them. Annette was a mom, a big, hairy mom, but still a mom. He knew she would like flowers, too.

He pulled seven or eight of the bright yellow blooms from the ground and arranged them in a bunch. He ran back to Annette and found her sitting in the same spot, holding Froggums against her cheek.

"You like Froggums, don't you?" Evan Nestor said. "He's soft. But he's mine. You have to give him back now."

Annette nodded. She handed Froggums back to Evan Nestor.

"Uuuu dnnn't shrrrr," she said.

"I picked these for you." He handed the yellow bouquet to Annette, who took them and nodded her thanks. "My mom likes it when I give her flowers."

Annette sniffed the flowers, and then, to Evan Nestor's surprise, she pushed the whole bunch into her mouth and began to slowly chew them.

"Hey, they weren't to eat..." Evan Nestor began.

Then he shrugged. "Oh well, they're yours. You can eat them if you want to."

Annette yawned. She had seemed sleepy all day, and Evan Nestor thought she must usually sleep during the day but was changing her normal ways to take care of him.

"Ssllllppp nnwww," Annette said. "Tkkk rrrvvnnn t... t... rdd tmmmrrrwww."

"Take me to the road tomorrow," Evan Nestor repeated. Annette nodded. She crawled into the nest she had made and lay on her right side. Evan Nestor crawled into the nest, too, and after an awkward moment puzzling about where to position himself, he lay on his right side also, against Annette's chest.

As soon as he had settled in, the low growl could be heard again, drifting down from the hillside behind them. The growl grew into a fierce, cat-like scream. Evan Nestor sat up quickly, looking out into the gathering darkness and holding Froggums close to him. He felt an enormous hand pick him up by the back and shoulders of his T-shirt. Gently, Annette lifted him and set him down behind her, between her back and the wall of the nest.

"Sfff thrrr," she said. "Slllpppp."

Chapter 14

When Evan Nestor awoke the next morning, he found himself alone in the nest. He clutched Froggums tightly as he sat up and looked toward the river. The sun was just coming up over the high hills to the east, and the mist, now quickly disappearing in the warm sunlight, hung like ghosts over the few quiet patches of water on the opposite bank.

There, as still as a boulder or a tree trunk, stood Annette, knee-deep in water, watching for a fish to catch. Evan Nestor watched quietly. Then suddenly, as quick as lightning, Annette plunged her hand into the water and pulled out a wriggling trout. She threw the fish onto the riverbank behind her, then quickly plunged her hand into the water a second time and caught another fish, which she dropped onto the ground alongside the first one, under a small spruce tree.

She then grasped the tree trunk about six feet from the ground and twisted it until it shredded like an unraveling rope. She bent the broken top of the tree down and pointed it at the spot where she had caught the fish. Annette picked up the two fish from the ground and crossed the shallow river back toward the nest. She then sat on a boulder on the pebbly beach a few feet from Evan Nestor. In a few minutes, she had several strips of the pink trout laid out on a flat rock nearby. She looked over her right shoulder and motioned to Evan Nestor.

"I'm not hungry," Evan Nestor frowned.

"Shdd utt," Annette said. "Utt."

"Ok, I'll eat a little." Evan Nestor shrugged. He walked out onto the beach and picked up a strip of the fish from the rock. He had to admit, it tasted pretty good, and he was hungrier than he thought. "This tastes like sushi. My mom likes it, but Dad don't. He hates it."

Annette ate her fish quickly and then swished her hands in the stream in front of her. She then stood and pointed toward a steep hillside to the southwest.

"Thsss wwww."

Evan Nestor understood. He also washed his hands in the stream and began to walk in the direction Annette had pointed.

"Frrggg...frrggg," Annette said, and she picked up Froggums from the ground where Evan Nestor had left him.

"Do you want to carry Froggums for a while?" Evan Nestor said.

Annette nodded and smiled a broad smile.

As they walked along the riverbank, the blue and pink and gray stones made smooth by the river crunched under their feet. Soon the stones gave way to soft mud, and as Evan Nestor ran alongside Annette, trying to keep up, he looked behind them and noticed how odd her enormous footprints looked next to his small ones. Soon, their walking had a rhythm to it and Evan Nestor found it easier to keep pace with her.

He looked behind them a second time, and as he

was glancing back, he saw how every time Annette took a step beside him, her tree trunk legs made a large, crooked triangle shape that was taller than Evan Nestor himself. After watching it a moment, he wondered if he could run through this gap and not get bumped by her knee swinging forward. Watching for his chance, and to Annette's surprise, Evan Nestor suddenly dived through the bent triangle space and skidded to a stop in the mud on the other side.

Annette looked down at him, perplexed at first, but when he giggled, she giggled, and Evan Nestor quickly ran back through the space again. He did this, back and forth, as Annette walked, and he noticed that she even seemed to slow down her pace a bit, so he had a little more time to make it through. The mud soon gave way to gravel again as they headed into the woods.

It was slow going up the hillside and Evan Nestor was quickly exhausted. Annette saw this. She tapped him on the head and motioned that he could ride on her shoulder. He nodded, and she lifted him up into position, and he held on for dear life.

After climbing for an hour or so, the spruce and cedar forest opened to a tiny meadow. There, Evan Nestor noticed, were two more small trees with the tops twisted and pointed toward the ground.

"Fdd hrrr," Annette said, "Ntts, mssrmmms."

"I don't want nuts or mushrooms," Evan Nestor winced. In the distance, a twig snapped. Annette lowered him to the ground. She put her hand over her mouth, which Evan Nestor knew meant to keep still and quiet.

Neither of them moved or made a sound for many minutes. After a while, Evan Nestor was sure he was hearing footsteps in the underbrush close by. Annette was looking at a spot on a rocky, moss-covered ridge in the direction of the footsteps, and Evan Nestor watched the spot also. Soon, against the dark tree trunks and specks of sunlight dancing on the ferns, a dark shape emerged. It took a moment for Evan Nestor to understand, but he realized he was looking at another Sasquatch!

The Sasquatch on the ridge was a large male with a gray beard. He seemed to be in a hurry, but when he spotted Annette and Evan Nestor, he stopped short.

"Hdddsssnnn," Annette said.

"Hudson?" Evan Nestor asked.

Annette nodded. She held both her arms out toward Hudson with the palms of her hands exposed to him. Hudson nodded in response. He looked at Annette for a long moment and made a sound deep down in his throat that Evan Nestor could feel, as well as hear. Hudson then swept his right arm away from himself and disappeared below the ridgeline.

"He had a look in his eye like he wanted to tell you something," Evan Nestor whispered.

Annette continued to watch the spot where Hudson had vanished with a troubled look on her face. She touched Evan Nestor's head and motioned for him to come with her and step behind the trunk of a large redwood tree. In another minute, Evan Nestor heard more footsteps in the woods, along with the sounds of men talking.

The sounds got louder and soon, two men were visible wearing camouflage hats and orange vests and carrying hunting rifles.

"I think it went this way," one of the men said. "It wasn't a bear. You know what I think it was!"

"No, wasn't a bear," the other man agreed. "Have your gun ready just in case."

Evan Nestor looked at the men for a moment, then at Annette's face. She seemed worried, and a bit frightened. She looked down at Evan Nestor and nodded toward the men, as if to say: "We can let these humans find you… if you want."

Evan Nestor moved, as quietly as he could do it, behind Annette and out of the sight of the hunters. She placed her enormous hand gently on his head, as if this would help him melt into her and be invisible. In a few minutes, the men were out of sight down the hill.

"Hvvvv tttt bbbb cccrrrffflll," Annette whispered.

"Careful," Evan Nestor agreed.

Annette pressed slightly on Evan Nestor's head for him to sit on the ground. He did.

"Styy hrrr," she said.

"What are you going to do?" Evan Nestor meant to whisper, but it came out as loud as his normal voice.

Annette did not respond. She stepped out quietly from behind the tree, looking in the direction Hudson and the two hunters had gone. Cupping her hands beside her mouth, she let out a piercing whistle followed by several deep, echoing whoops.

"What are you doing?" Evan Nestor said, almost in a panic. "Those mean men will come and get you!"

Annette smiled at him and shook her head no. She moved a few feet to her right, and facing north, made the sounds again.

"Holy guacamole," Evan Nestor thought. For all the world, it sounded as if the sounds were coming from some great distance away, and were heading toward Annette, not away from her!

"How did you do that?" Evan Nestor said.

In another second or two, sounds like Annette had made, but deeper, came back up the mountainside.

"Is that Hudson?" Evan Nestor was puzzled.

Annette nodded and smiled at him again. She stooped to the ground and picked up several good-sized rocks. With all her might, she threw these down the mountainside, one after the other. She did this several times, until Evan Nestor joined her, though the rocks he threw only went a few feet.

After a moment, Annette held out her hand for Evan Nestor to be still. In the distance, they could clearly hear the hunter's voices. They seemed to be in a panic.

"Gosh all fishhooks!" one man said, "we're surrounded!"

"Let's get outta here," the other man yelled. "South! South is the only way out!"

The sound of them stumbling and crashing through the brush could be heard for many minutes. Then, after the sounds of the hunters had finally faded away, two sharp whistles could be heard off in the distance. It must be Hudson again, Evan Nestor thought. Annette cupped her hands and whistled once in response. She then turned toward Evan Nestor and held out her hand.

"Go," she said.

Chapter 15

Wesley felt sleepy. Something sweet to eat would help. The emergency red licorice he had sewn into the lining of his vest had melted a little, and he had some trouble getting it out. The reserve chocolate-covered peanuts, mint drops, and the other sweets in little cardboard boxes were in better condition, and many had not been smashed in any way. Not that being smashed would make them something he wouldn't eat. No. He considered himself to be officially out of food, but he had enough emergency sweets to last a little while longer. And since three hikers had found him stuck in the bog and helped him get his ATV free of it, he decided to continue searching for his quarry.

Wesley's eyelids were heavy, but the tracking signal from the homing device had become stronger, showing that the Sasquatch was very close to him now. He would fight the urge to take a nap. It looked as though the creature was moving west toward Highway 96. Wesley figured the sheriff and Search and Rescue would approach that same area from the north and west. He would have to hurry if he was going to find the Sasquatch and little boy first.

The animal was too far away for a good thermal image, so he wasn't sure if the little boy was still with her. Wesley suspected he must be, though, because the Sasquatch was moving toward the highway where she was more likely to see people and to be seen by them. And, if she kept moving in a straight line southwest from where she was now, she could even get caught in one of the snare traps Wesley had placed a year ago that had never been sprung.

Luckily the forest floor was flat enough for Wesley to continue on his ATV. He should be able to make it all the way to the highway, he thought. Wesley's phone rang.

"What is it, Mom?"

"This is your mother. Just wanted to know if you got unst—"

"Mom, Mom, you hear the motor running, don't you? Would I run the motor if I was still stuck?"

"Well... I guess not..."

"I'm tracking the Sasquatch. There is a little lost boy with her. Search and Rescue are looking for him. I'm gonna find them both!"

"Wesley!" Juanita gasped, "You'll be a hero and a celebrity! A celebrity cryptozoologist!"

"Yes." Wesley smiled. "I'll be interviewed on TV, and in the newspaper, and maybe write a book. They'll make large coffee mugs and extra-large T-shirts with my picture on them... and maybe a Sasquatch in the background. Maybe I could even..."

"... even..." Juanita said with excitement growing in her voice.

"... even have a TV show: 'Buttinski's Crypto-Challenge.'"

Juanita was speechless for a moment.

"But son," she said at length, "what if the Sasquatch won't give up the boy? They are very protective mothers, you know. What if she has adopted him and protects him? How will you get him away from her?"

"She's going toward Highway 96. She must be taking him there so he can be found."

"Are you going to photograph her?"

"*Catch* her. She's headed right for some snare traps I set along the highway. If I can lure her in—"

"But why did you set traps on the highway? You won't catch an animal right on the highway like that."

"Mom, Mom, Mom, correct me if I'm wrong, but if I set a trap on the highway then I can get to it on my ATV, right? You can't always get everywhere in the woods on an ATV."

Just then Wesley saw a flash of gold in the sunlight off to his right and heard a low growl. He stopped his ATV. Looking into the pines and spruces, he could see a flicker of movement. A mountain lion!

It was moving in the same direction Wesley was, but it seemed uninterested in him. The lion stopped suddenly and fixed its gaze on something up ahead. Wesley heard the snap of a twig and the rustle of underbrush. He looked in the direction the lion was.

Along the hillside that led up to the highway, Wesley saw a bright patch of blond hair bobbing in the air. It was a little boy, but he was impossibly high off the ground. Wesley realized that the boy was sitting atop a large, dark shape, a huge mass of flesh that almost disappeared into the forest behind it.

It was the Sasquatch! Wesley's mouth was dry, but he managed a gulp.

"Mom... Mom... I'll call you back."

Chapter 16

The Krantz's Grove UFO Task Force had swung into action. Lester Mann, the president and executive director, and Global Chief Executive Officer, carried one of several parabolic dishes. His wife, Dot, wore earphones with an antenna and had a laptop computer strapped to herself on which she read signals from the dish. The ten or twelve other members of the group who followed them carried similar equipment, some of it new, some of it taped and patched together, showing the effects of years of use. The entire group wore aluminum foil on their heads. The task force had gone on alert when a flock of geese flew over, but other than that, they had not seen or heard anything noteworthy.

Sheriff Fletcher, Megan, and Duane had been with Deputy Clark's team when the two groups met at Bluff Creek near the highway. Now they had word that Search and Rescue, coming in from the northeast and led by bloodhounds, was heading their way.

"Looks like we're all going to come together at the highway," Clark noted.

"Hope we find him soon," Duane said.

"Getting any magnetic pulse readings, Lester?" Sheriff Fletcher asked.

"None." Lester shook his head. "They're really hiding their tracks this time."

The sheriff shook his head. "Pretty crafty, them exa-tressials! But we've got the people, and we've got the tuknology!"

Deputy Clark was on his walkie-talkie. "Okay, that's good news," he said. "Over and out." He looked at Duane and Megan. "Bloodhounds have been following a scent. We'll see S and R in maybe ten minutes."

"That's good!" Megan said. "It must be him! It's something at least!"

***

Wesley had gone as far as his ATV would go. He would have to climb a small hillside to get any closer to the highway. He could still see the mountain lion creeping through the ferns below him, watching the movements of the little boy.

Wesley slid out of the ATV as quietly as he could, though he grunted loudly, and the skin of his thighs screeched across his plastic seat cover. And as he stepped out onto the ground, he fell and rolled down the hillside a few feet.

But neither the mountain lion nor the Sasquatch, he thought... he was *sure*... had noticed him. He started to climb slowly back up the hillside, steadying himself on oak and spruce saplings as he went. It was a cool day, but Wesley was soon covered in sweat. And he was starving.

He could see the Sasquatch ahead of him with the little boy on her shoulders, climbing the same hillside a few hundred feet away. Looking a little further to the east, he saw the mountain lion. But now, Wesley saw, the lion was looking right at him.

***

Annette felt strong beneath Evan Nestor, but he could tell she was a little out of breath. As they climbed the hillside, he could see a cleared, open area above them, and he knew this must be the highway.

Suddenly Annette stopped and looked back into the woods to the left of them. They heard a snapping branch, a grunt, and someone saying, "Ohhhhhh!" Following the sound, Evan Nestor saw a very fat man in shorts and camouflage picking himself up off the ground.

"There's a person over there," Evan Nestor said urgently." He'll see you! He might see you!"

After a moment, Annette said, "Hmmmffff," and continued to climb the hill.

In another few seconds, she stopped and turned to her left again. There in the shadows was the mountain lion, still following them. Evan Nestor could see that now the lion was approaching the fat man.

Wesley was back on his feet with some difficulty. He continued up the hill. Yes, the area was familiar. It was one of the spots on the highway where he had placed the snares.

At the top of the hill was a small flat area covered in oaks, pine, and spruce, and just beyond that was Highway 96.

Wesley's stomach was growling. He needed to get closer to the spot where the Sasquatch would come out onto the road. He removed his stun gun from his vest pocket. He would stun the animal, then photograph it with his digital camera. He wasn't so sure about trying to actually capture the animal by himself anymore. She was so big he might need help for that, and she wouldn't fit on his ATV. He hoped the stun gun had enough juice to do the trick. He had taken it off charge on Thursday to plug in his blender to make a smoothie and never plugged it back in. He had to admit to himself that he hadn't planned this out as well as he thought he had.

Wesley stopped to catch his breath. He was in a glade about thirty feet from the highway. He thought he could hear helicopters far off somewhere and dogs barking in the distance. He figured the search teams were heading his way. His stomach growled again.

Suddenly, right in front of him, he saw it: a snare trap he had set nearly a year ago. And though he could hardly believe it, it was still baited.

There on the ground in front of him was the packet of golden Twonky cakes, the snack that never spoils and lasts forever. They should still taste great, Wesley thought. He knew he should leave them alone, but he stepped forward to pick them up.

Sproing!

The trap sprung tight, and Wesley found himself upside down, bouncing in the air. He unwrapped the Twonky package and took a bite.

He heard, or thought he heard, a low growl behind him on the hillside. He might have imagined it because he sometimes imagined things when he was hungry. Wesley felt a little angry at himself because he realized, as he swallowed the last morsel of cake, that he was getting very sleepy.

Chapter 17

By the time they got to the glade, Annette and Evan Nestor could hear many sounds: dogs barking, the sound of helicopters in the distance, and a puzzling noise coming from much closer that sounded a lot like snoring.

"Dgggss," Annette said, looking toward the north.

"Yeah, dogs," Evan Nestor repeated. "Sounds like the kind of dogs that smell your clothes then find you when you're lost. They're looking for me..." Evan Nestor thought for a minute. "But... they can't find you. If they find me, they might find you. They'll try to catch you and take you away. If Aidan Connor comes back, he'll never be able to find you! You... you'll have to leave me here."

There was worry in Evan Nestor's voice, and Annette smiled her odd smile. She lifted him off her shoulders and placed him on the ground.

"Cnnnntt fnnnndd Uunnnttt," she said.

"Can't find Annette!" Evan Nestor said earnestly. "That's the most important thing."

Annette looked down at the tiny boy affectionately. There was a tear on his cheek, but Evan Nestor's attention suddenly focused on something very odd behind Annette at a bend in the road. It was the source of the snoring sound, something that looked at first like an enormous Christmas tree ornament bobbing on a branch. It was the very fat man he'd seen a minute ago, but now he was dangling from a snare trap.

And just below the hefty man, looking ready to jump, was the mountain lion.

"*Rrrrrrkkkkkk!*" yowled Annette, waving her arms.

The lion looked at her, startled, and froze for a minute. But soon the big cat returned its attention to Wesley, and steadied itself again, to jump.

In addition to the sounds of the dogs barking and the helicopter hovering, Evan Nestor now thought he could hear people talking.

"*RRRRRRRRRRRRR!*" Annette howled and ran toward the lion. Wesley was snoring even more loudly now. The lion roared at Annette and arched its back.

Annette stopped suddenly and looked back at Evan Nestor, as if she wondered if he would be safe when she chased the big cat away from the dangling, snoring man. Could she get back to Evan Nestor before the lion did?

"Go on," Evan Nestor yelled, waving Froggums at her. "I'm okay!"

Annette turned again, and waving her arms, ran right for the mountain lion. Angrily, the lion arched its back again, roared, and ran off to the south toward Bluff Creek, disappearing among the evergreens and ferns.

Standing under Wesley, Annette reached as far over her head as she could and grabbed his chubby arm. She looked back at Evan Nestor, a few hundred feet away: he was watching her anxiously. Then she looked in the direction the lion had run but saw no sign of it. It seemed to have truly run off this time, but with a lion, you can never be sure.

The sounds of dogs and people were even louder now. Then a black helicopter appeared over the trees to the north. It was going from west to east and didn't seem to have seen them yet.

Evan Nestor was determined that the people and dogs must *not* find Annette. He looked at her holding the very fat sleeping man off the ground, which appeared to be taking all her strength, while she attempted to chew through the rope that was holding his ankle.

"I'm okay!" Evan Nestor yelled at Annette. "I'm gonna be okay!"

Evan Nestor saw that Annette was watching him. He waved at her then turned north on the highway and began to run toward a sharp bend just ahead. He knew she could see the helicopter in the air and hear the dogs and people close by. He knew that now she was sure that in a few moments he would be safe.

But he was not sure where the mountain lion was, and the heavy human Annette was holding would not be safe from it until he woke up. Annette chewed and gnawed, and in another few seconds, the rope holding the sleeping man snapped.

Annette wrapped her arms around Wesley's chest, and, as carefully as she could manage it, carried him back down the hillside and into the woods.

Glancing over his shoulder, Evan Nestor saw her head disappear below the edge of the glade floor.

Chapter 18

In a few seconds, Evan Nestor had run around the bend in the mountain road and could no longer see Annette. The helicopter he had seen before circled back and now hovered about one hundred feet above him. He waved at it. Another helicopter flew in from the west, hovered for a moment, then landed on a gravel turnout further north on the road. Two men got out of it, one carrying a first aid kit, the other, an oxygen tank. In another minute, three bloodhounds, barking and pulling the men who held onto their leashes, appeared from the tree line. Behind them, Evan Nestor saw what he wanted more than anything to see: his mom and dad!

When Duane and Megan saw Evan Nestor, they ran toward him with smiles on their faces and tears in their eyes.

"Son! Son! You're safe... you're safe!" Megan shouted. In a second her arms were around him, and Duane's were around both of them.

"Oh, son!" Duane said. "I'm so sorry we lost you. We're so glad you're safe!"

"You didn't lose me, Dad, I lost myself!"

"But how did you make it here? Where did you sleep?" Megan asked excitedly. "Did you eat anything?"

Evan Nestor thought about it for a moment. "I'll tell you about it... soon," he said. "In a little while." He wrapped his arms around his father's neck and hugged him. "Dad, there are more things in the world than we know about, than you know about. But I'll tell you about them later."

Evan Nestor realized they were surrounded by people. There was the deputy and the men from the helicopter, and there were the men with the bloodhounds, and many more people who had followed them. And there were lots of people, including Sheriff Fletcher, who carried laptops and had aluminum foil on their heads. One of these men, who seemed to be their leader, took an electronic wand out of his backpack, switched it on, and passed it slowly over Evan Nestor.

"No sign of implants, Sheriff," the man said.

"Good," Sheriff Fletcher said. "But we'll see what the doctors say when they check him over."

The two men from the helicopter carrying the first-aid kit and oxygen approached Duane, Megan, and Evan Nestor.

"Son," Megan said, "these men are going to check you for cuts and scrapes, and then we're going to take you to the hospital just to have a doctor look at you."

"I'm okay, Mom."

"You're not hungry? You should be starving."

"No Mom, I'm full. We ate all the time!"

"'We?' What do you mean 'we,' son?" Duane said.

Evan Nestor looked at his dad and grinned.

"Dad," he said, "take me over there." He nodded toward the side of the road which dropped off sharply into the woods. Duane looked puzzled, but took Evan Nestor from Megan and carried him to the shoulder of the road. They stood, looking down into the woods.

"Lift me over your head, Dad," Evan Nestor said, and Duane did as his son asked, though he was a big enough boy now that it wasn't easy anymore.

As hard and as far as he could manage it, Evan Nestor threw Froggums into the woods. Duane was shocked.

"Son!" Duane said, "Why did you do that? Froggums was your favorite toy. The thing that made you feel safe. You wanted to keep him..."

"It's a present, Dad." Evan Nestor looked for many moments at Froggums lying below them on the pine needles. Duane looked, too.

"A present?" he asked.

Then, out of the shadows and ferns, an enormous shape appeared, hair-covered and massive. Duane could not believe what he was seeing. The giant form reached down and picked up the stuffed green toy. A face, dark and unclear, but kind, smiled at them from the gloom, then, as her people had done in the presence of humans for thousands of years, vanished among the tree trunks.

Duane was absolutely and utterly speechless. He lowered Evan Nestor to his chest and hugged him tightly.

"I will tell you about things, Dad," Evan Nestor said. "I will tell you about many things... soon... And Dad..."

Duane, perplexed and bewildered, looked at his son.

"Dad," Evan Nestor continued, and he said it in a very ordinary way, as though nothing very interesting had yet happened in his life, "you owe Mom five dollars."

Author's Note

My interest in this subject was inevitable. Like Evan Nestor Bettancourt, I was a kid who loved monsters. But my trigger for the case of Bigfoot was my grandmother.

When I was nine or ten, my grandparents lived on a farm in Hopewell, Missouri. It was an isolated forty acres, all red clay, boulders, and scrub cedars. Distances between neighbors were measured in miles, not feet. Every summer I was expected to spend a week or so at the farm, helping grandma wherever I could, and keeping her company.

She normally spent her days alone with no company but Rex, the old, black-and-white collie who chased rabbits and occasionally killed black snakes. Grandma cleaned house incessantly, canned fruit and vegetables, did laundry that she hung on a line in the back yard to dry, said her rosary, and listened to the radio. The radio station was considered local but originated in far off Potosi, or "Flat River." I remember the droning voice of the announcer, with a southern Missouri country accent reading farm news, livestock prices, and who was expecting out-of-town visitors this week. Pretty boring days for me.

My grandpa was still working then, as a blacksmith in the lead mines. I knew when he came home from work at three o'clock every day, there would be some variety in the routine: feeding livestock, going to get clean, fresh water from the spring, or just going for a drive. Every afternoon, I waited at the end of the drive at the old gravel road for him to get home.

Occupying myself until three p.m. was a challenge. Luckily, my grandmother saved magazines. I don't remember if it was *Life* or *Look* or, more likely, some lesser adventure magazine, but I came across an article, luridly illustrated, about giant, human-like footprints that had been found a few years before by roadcrews working near Willow Creek, California. Not only were enormous footprints found, but the crews reported heavy steel drums and earth-mover tires being moved around at night. The story was illustrated with a thrilling depiction of a hairy monster running across a highway to the horror and disbelief of workers in the distance. From then on, I was hooked. As far as Bigfoot went, there was no turning back for me.

Imagine my excitement to learn from an older cousin years later that my great-great grandfather Larkin, also a blacksmith, was attacked one night in the woods as he rode his mule home from a horse-shoeing job at a neighboring farm. The creature, nothing Larkin had ever seen before, jumped onto the mule behind Grandpa, but together, he and the mule fought it off.

Annette: A Big, Hairy Mom was inspired by a feature in the *New York Times Style Magazine* of March 27, 2011. In a story profiling Humboldt County, California, a lady told the reporter the account of a four-year-old boy who was lost in the woods. She was one of the volunteers at the Willow

Creek China Flat Museum in Willow Creek, which houses the artifacts of decades of Bigfoot contact in the area. When the boy was found, he told his rescuers he was saved by a hairy giant who took him to a highway where he could be found by humans. This struck me as a storyline I wanted to develop.

My son and I visited those ladies at Willow Creek a few years ago. We heard their stories and saw their artifacts. Thanks to them for their very cheerful and matter-of-fact accounts of the hairy giants, and to everyone we encountered on the Redwood Coast for whom the existence of Bigfoot is not such an extraordinary fact of life.

In addition, many thanks to my editor, Andrea Thomas, who made this tale a tighter, more coherent story.

John S. McFarland
February 2022

ANNETTE:
A Big, Hairy Grandma
Coming soon!

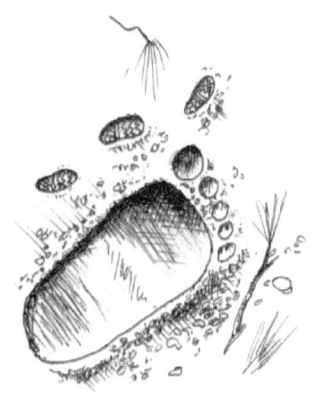

About the Author

Iohn S. McFarland's first adult novel, *The Black Garden*, was published in 2010 to universal praise. His work has appeared in *The Twilight Zone Magazine, Eldritch Tales, National Lampoon, River Styx, Tornado Alley*, and in the anthology *A Treasury of American Horror Stories*. He has written extensively on historical and arts-related subjects and has been a guest lecturer in fiction at Washington University in St. Louis. He is a lifelong Bigfoot enthusiast, and *Annette: A Big, Hairy Mom* is his first novel for young readers.

SPOOKY SHORT TALES
TO CHILL YOU TO YOUR BONES!

Vonnie's creepy stories written just for Kids combined with her vivid illustrations are perfect for reading under the covers with your flashlight!

Grayson North can't catch a break.

That is,
until he inherits a silvery key with copper bands.
He suddenly gains wintery superpowers
and a world of epic responsibility.
He must protect the City of Chicago from the firey
extra-dimensional monsters known as Sulfurians.

But can he master his powers and uncover
the Sulfurians' plans to bring back the
Great Chicago Fire before it's too late?

Grayson North
Frost-Keeper
of the Windy City

by

Kevin M. Folliard

Available in paperback and on Kindle
www.darkowlpublishing.com

COME TO DARK OWL'S WEBSITE
AND VISIT

The
Young Readers
Bookstore

OUR CURRENT AND UPCOMING YOUNG
READER BOOKS ARE FOR A VARIETY OF
READING LEVELS!

**And we rate the age appropriateness of all
Dark Owl's books on our website.**

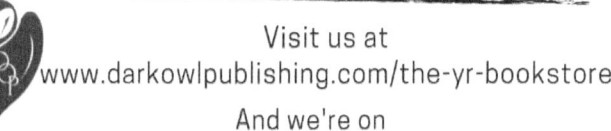

Visit us at
www.darkowlpublishing.com/the-yr-bookstore

And we're on

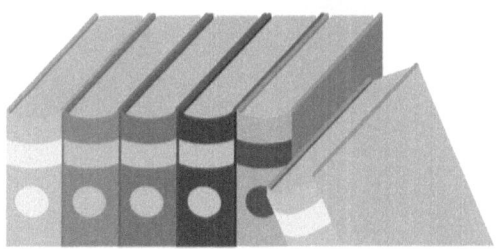